This SCRIBBLERS
book belongs to:

....

This edition published in Great Britain in MMXIX
by Scribblers, an imprint of
The Salariya Book Company Ltd
25 Marlborough Place,
Brighton BN1 1UB
www.salariya.com

SALARIYA
SCRIBO BOOK HOUSE SCRIBBLERS

© Editions Langue Au Chat - BELGIUM
English language © The Salariya Book Company Ltd MMXVIII

HB ISBN-13: 978-1-912006-85-4
PB ISBN-13: 978-1-912537-38-9

1 3 5 7 9 8 6 4 2

A CIP catalogue record for this book is
available from the British Library.

Printed and bound in China

Printed on paper from sustainable sources

Visit
www.salariya.com
for our online catalogue and
free fun stuff.

Marie Tibi is a writer and illustrator, specialising in
picture books for young readers. She also travels to
schools to give art workshops. She lives near
Aix-en-Provence in the south of France with
her family.

Fabien Öckto Lambert is a graphic designer,
illustrator and writer of children's books. He lives in
Nantes in France.

Little Bear

Jules

Oswald

Big Deer

Sally

Bill

Sammy

It was a cold and snowy day in Four Seasons Wood. All the animals were excited about Christmas and the presents they hoped Santa Claus would bring them.

'I've written to Santa Claus and asked for a new coat,' said Sally the stoat.
Jules, the white rabbit, licked his lips. 'I've asked for a pot of carrot jam! Or a new pair of boots.'
'Oh, I'd love a sketchbook and some sharp new pencils,' said Sammy the skunk.

They chatted happily about their letters to Santa Claus and the magical night that was less than one month away.

The woodland friends all had a lovely time as they toasted marshmallows and made Christmas plans about what to eat and how to decorate their nests, caves and burrows.

All except one.

'Hey Little Bear, why are you looking so glum? Don't you like Christmas?' asked Big Deer.

Little Bear sighed. 'Christmas isn't for me; I'll be going to bed soon for my long winter sleep, and once again I'll miss this magical time of year. What's the point in decorating my cave when I'll be asleep hibernating until the spring? What's the point in writing a letter to Santa Claus when he'll go straight past my door without leaving a present?'

With a heavy heart, Little Bear
walked slowly home.

Oswald the wise owl explained, 'Yes, it's true, bears go to sleep before the big freeze comes and they don't wake up until the warm days of spring arrive.

Oh dear, poor Little Bear, surely there is something we can do to help him experience the magic and wonder of Christmas?'

Then Bill the badger had a fantastic idea!
'Why don't we celebrate an Almost Christmas,
just before Little Bear goes away to hibernate?'
Of course, all the friends agreed at once.
'That's the spirit of Christmas, it's for everyone!
Giving, sharing, and spreading joy!
Shall we make it a surprise?'

The friends got to work. Each of them would bring something special to make Little Bear's Almost Christmas truly magical! A crown of pinecones, a garland of feathers, a soft blanket of moss. They brought lanterns, an enormous honey cake and a twinkling star. This was going to be the best Almost Christmas celebration ever!

The next morning, Big Deer went to see Little Bear. 'Let's go for a walk, Little Bear,' he said. 'I've spotted a bush in the woods bursting with juicy berries!'

Greedy Little Bear jumped at the idea, and off they went. Little did he know that meanwhile his friends were busy decorating his house and getting everything ready for the big surprise.

'Quick, they're on their way back! Is everything ready?' called Sally.

MERRY

Yes! Everything was perfect,
even the banner:
MERRY ALMOST
CHRISTMAS!

Ta-da!

ALMOST CHRISTMAS

What a wonderful surprise!

That night in Four Seasons Wood
a very happy Little Bear celebrated
his first ever Almost Christmas
with all his special friends.

As he settled down for his big sleep, Little Bear looked forward to lots of sweet dreams about his Almost Christmas.

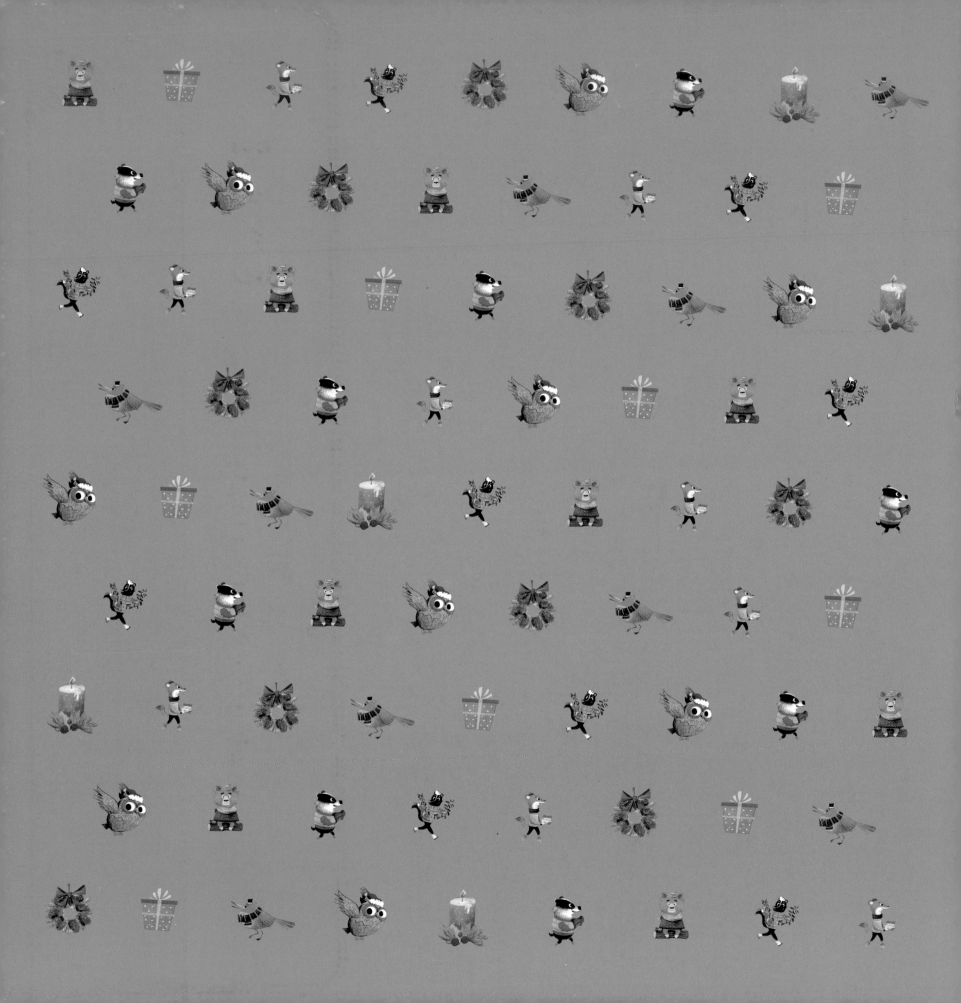